A

BEST FRIENDS DO

Will and Rosa Meet the Grandreaders

WRITTEN BY
Ann Jackman & Terrie Manchester

ILLUSTRATED BY
Amy Jackman

Self-Published
Available for retail through Amazon.com

First Edition 2020

This book is a work of fiction. Names, characters, places, and incidents either are the
product of the authors' imagination or used fictitiously, and any resemblance to
actual persons, living or dead, is entirely coincidental.

ISBN: 978-0-578-73524-5

THIS BOOK
IS DEDICATED TO:

*The Jewish Council for the
Aging of Greater Washington, founders of the
awesome Grandreaders program;*

*Bill, Rosemary, and all those involved in
Grandreaders; and*

*Amy & Zoe, whose time and talent
helped make our idea a reality.*

CHAPTER ONE

SCHOOL BEGINS

The Children

On a beautiful September morning, Rosa and Will were standing at the corner of Main Street. They meet every morning to walk to school together, *as best friends do*. Today, they have something special to talk about.

"Miss Benjamin told me yesterday that next week I will be part of a new program. It is called Grandreaders. Did your teacher tell you about it?" asked Rosa.

"Yes, she did. And I'm very worried. Do you know what it's about and why we have to go?" said Will.

"Miss Benjamin told me we will spend time reading with a partner, and I'm really excited to go because I love books! Why are you so worried?"

"Since you ask, here are just a few of the reasons I'm scared. Does this mean more work? Will we miss recess? Suppose the teacher is grumpy? Does this mean I'm not smart? And anyway, what's so important about books?"

As they approached the school, Rosa remained excited about Grandreaders, but Will remained worried.

❦ The Adults ❦

On a beautiful September morning, Miss A and Miss T were talking on the phone, *as best friends do*.

"So, next week will be our first experience as volunteer Grandreaders. I know some students who are really smart just need a little extra attention, but I'm nervous. Are you as worried as I am?" said Miss A.

"No - I'm really looking forward to sharing my love of books with the children. Tell me why you're nervous," replied Miss T.

"Well, I have some questions. For example, will my student like me? Can I make a difference? Will the other Grandreaders make more progress with their student? Do you think we are too old?"

"I think if we all just try our best, it will be a wonderful year! See you next week."

CHAPTER TWO

THE FOLLOWING
WEEK

The Children

As Will closed the Grandreader classroom door, he smiled his secret smile at Rosa, *as best friends do*.

"Hey Will, what did you think of our first day of Grandreaders? I LOVED it! My Grandreader is Miss A and she is so kind! What about you?" said Rosa.

"You know, I was a little fearful, but I didn't have to be. Miss T, my Grandreader, seems to really care about me. We read a book about animals, and my Grandreader helped me to understand some words I didn't know. Actually it was fun figuring out new vocabulary words!" replied Will.

"Miss A wrote some of my new words on flashcards and we played a game with them. She gave me a set to keep and I am going to study them at home. I wonder how many flashcards I will have by the end of the year?" said Rosa.

"I bet I get one hundred!"

"That would be so cool!"

"What is cool," said Will, "is that there is no homework and my Grandreader loved teaching me new words and discussing the story with me."

"I can't wait to see what we'll read next week," said Rosa.

"You know what - I'm pretty excited too!"

The Adults

As the children closed the Grandreader classroom door, Miss A smiled happily at Miss T, *as best friends do.*

"What a great day!" said Miss T. "I just love my student and this program! What did you think?"

"You know, I was so nervous but I didn't have to be. My student, Rosa, was a delight to teach, and she is really smart.

She learned five new words today already," said Miss A.

"My student was quiet at first, but by the end of the hour he seemed really happy to be there. He asked great questions, and we had a chance to get to know one another. It turns out we both love football!"

"My student loves pizza, just like I do," added Miss A.

"I can't wait to come back next week," said Miss T happily. "Don't you just love Grandreaders?"

CHAPTER THREE

BEFORE WINTER BREAK

The Children

On a cold December day, Will and Rosa were walking home from school. Will waved hello to their neighbor's snowman and the children both giggled, *as best friends do*.

"So," said Will, "tomorrow is our last day of Grandreaders before winter break. I'm going to miss it."

"Me too," said Rosa. "I have learned so much from Miss A."

"I already have fifty-three flashcards. How many do you have?" asked Will.

"I haven't counted them, I just like reading them."

"You know what's funny - at the beginning of the year I spoke in a whisper. Now I'm not afraid to read out loud," said Will.

"Sometimes I read to my little brother and I pretend I'm his Grandreader. It's fun!"

"That's a great idea! I'm going to try that, too. Also, my mom promised that over the vacation I could get new reading books of my own to keep at home," said Will.

Just then, Rosa turned and waved goodbye to their neighbor's snowman, and the children both giggled some more and ran home.

The Adults

On a cold December day, Miss A and Miss T were taking a walk in the snow, *as best friends do*.

"I can't believe we are ready for winter break. I will miss Rosa," said Miss A.

"I'm excited," said Miss T, "because Will told me he will be getting some new reading books over the vacation. He told me he thinks books are great, and that's another thing we have in common."

"My student told me she pretends she's a Grandreader. That made me so happy," said Miss A.

They kept walking in the snow and talking on their way home.

CHAPTER FOUR

SPRING

The Children

Spring had arrived, and Will and Rosa were looking forward to the school book fair.

"I'm very excited because my mom said I could buy a new book this year," said Rosa.

Will answered, "Would you believe that I'm excited too? I think I might look for a book about planets. I just read one about

Earth with Miss T, and it was a higher level reading book! I can't wait to learn more!"

Rosa added, "I hope there are journals for sale."

"What's a journal?" Will asked.

"It's a special book where you can write your own thoughts. Miss A said I'm a really good writer and I believe her!"

"Will you ever write about me in your journal?"

"That's my little secret," said Rosa, and they both laughed, *as best friends do.*

·❦· The Adults ·❦·

Spring had arrived, and Miss A and Miss T were talking about the upcoming book fair.

"I'm so excited about the school book fair, and curious about what our students will choose there," said Miss A.

Miss T replied, "Me too. Will and I just finished a book about Earth, and he was so interested that I'm thinking he might want a non-fiction book about the planets."

"I think Rosa might look for a journal. I have been encouraging her to write more and more, and she seems to love the idea of writing her thoughts down. I know I do!" said Miss A.

Miss T had another thought. "I am so thrilled by the improvement our students have shown in reading. I was told by Will's classroom teacher that he has advanced two whole reading levels this year. Wow!"

Miss A said, "I wonder if Rosa will write about me in her journal?"

Miss T smiled and replied, "That will be her little secret!"

Miss A and Miss T laughed, *as best friends do*.

CHAPTER FIVE

THE END OF THE YEAR

The Children

On a beautiful June morning, Rosa and Will were together at recess.

"You look sad today, Will," said Rosa.

"I am a little sad because today was our last visit with our Grandreaders. Remember how worried I was about starting Grandreaders? Now I'm worried about finishing Grandreaders!"

"Oh Will," said Rosa. "Don't worry. We have learned so much this year from Miss A and Miss T."

"But they won't be with us next year."

"It doesn't matter," said Rosa. "After all, we are both reading so much better now, and we are both really smart!"

"I know, but Miss T is my friend and I will miss her. She is really my first older friend. Did you realize she is older than my grandmother?"

"It's OK, Will. We will see them around the school next year and they will still be our friends, but they will be helping next year's lucky second graders."

"I guess. What's been your favorite part of Grandreaders?" asked Will.

"My journal. I was able to write in it when my mom and I went to Spain to visit our cousins this year. How about you?"

"I liked that I got more flashcards than you did!"

And they gave each other a high five, *as best friends do.*

The Adults

As Will and Rosa walked toward the swings, Miss A and Miss T watched them from the window.

"I can't believe this was our last day of Grandreaders. Remember how nervous you were at the beginning of the year? Well, you needn't have worried, this year was wonderful!" said Miss T.

"I agree," said Miss A. "Will and Rosa are such great children and such a joy to teach."

"I know they will shine next year. It makes me smile to think how excited Will was about his flashcards. I think he is planning on sharing them with his younger siblings."

"I found out that Rosa did write about me in her journal, and that makes me smile too," said Miss A.

"I do hope we sometimes see Will and Rosa around the school next year. It will be fun to hear how things are going for our young friends."

And as they walked out of the building, they gave each other a high five, *as best friends do.*

Today's Lesson

-Reading is fun

-Books are forever friends

-We are all smart in our own way

-Friends come in all sizes and ages

-Worrying isn't the answer, confidence is

-Everyone has a story to write - what's yours?

THE END

The Jewish Council for the Aging of Greater Washington provides a variety of vibrant intergenerational programs, including the popular Grandreaders program, through its JCA Heyman Interages ® Center.

Dedicated older adult volunteers have been significantly impacting the lives of children here for more than 30 years, providing support and empathy as mentors and positive role models in schools and elsewhere.

For more information about all current JCA programs, please visit **accessjca.org** or email **interagesinfo@accessjca.org**.

Made in the USA
Coppell, TX
26 June 2021

58119741R00029